ANGIE MORGAN trained in Graphic Design and Illustration at
Goldsmith's College, London. She uses pastels and watercolour with collage
for her illustrations, working with scanned fabrics and textures.
Her inspiration comes from her three children, now grown up, and from
the children at her local primary school where she gives Maths and
Literacy support. Angie is also the writer and illustrator of *Enormouse*,
for Frances Lincoln Children's Books. She lives in Bath.

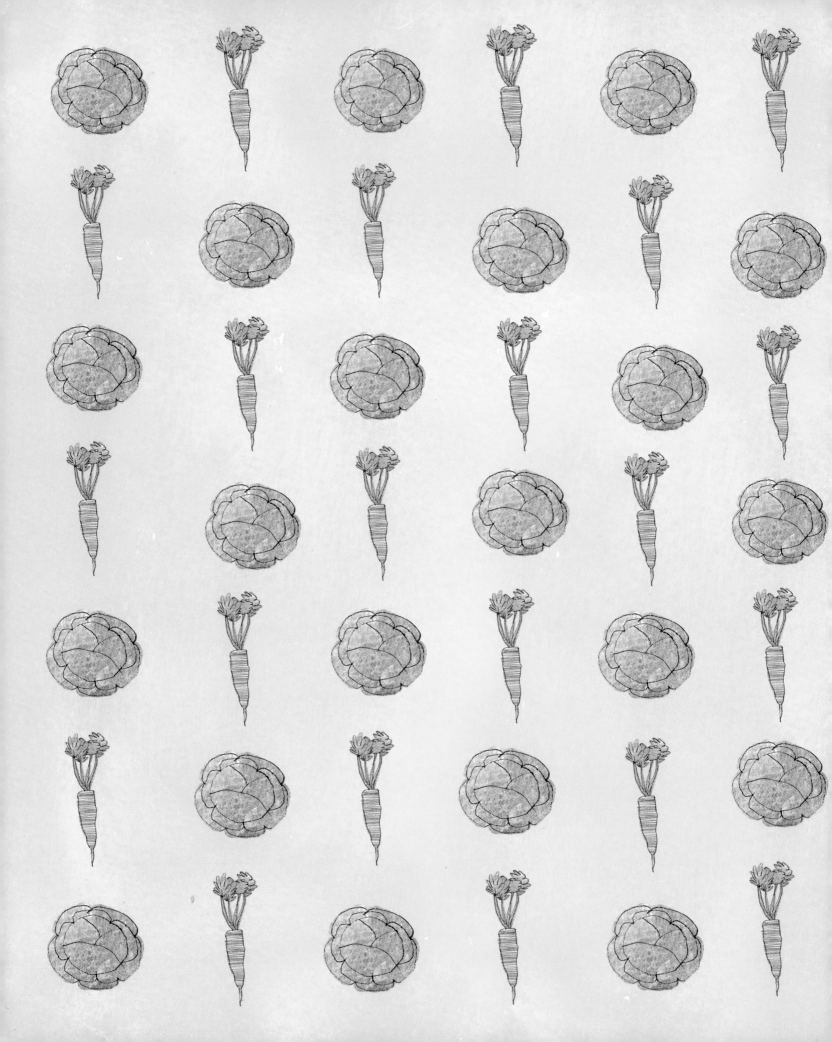

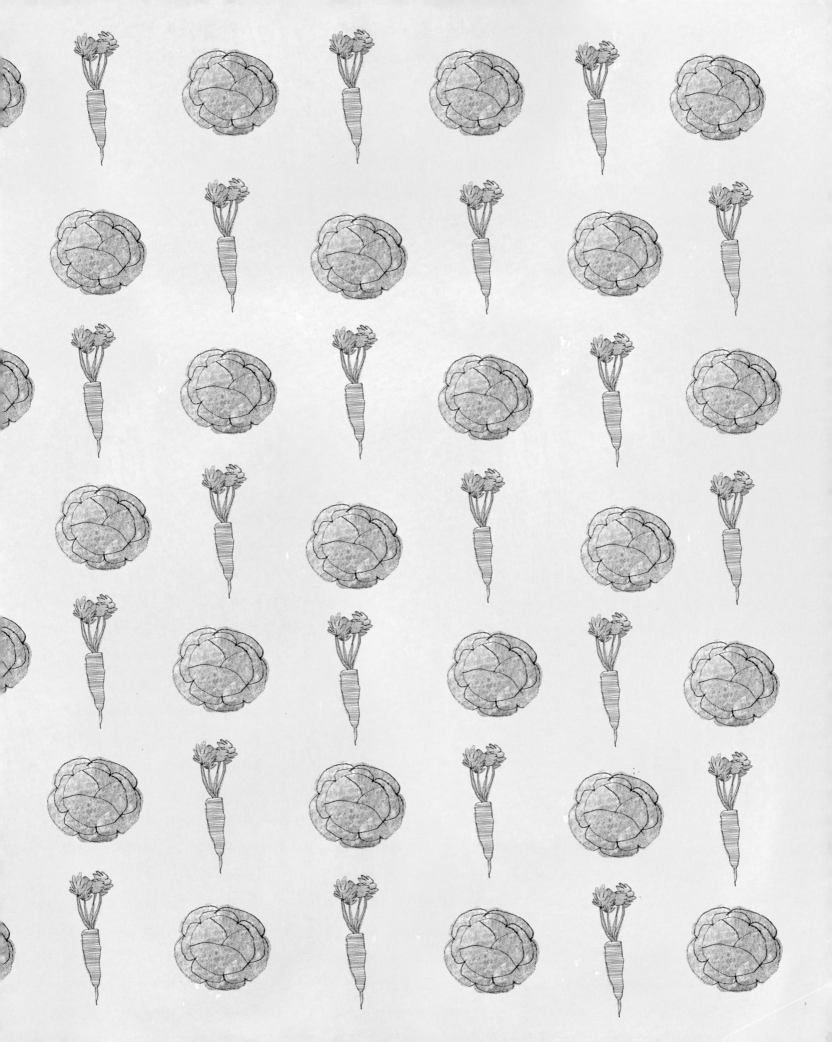

For
Gray
emily
Luke and
hannah
(with Love)

JANETTA OTTER-BARRY BOOKS

First published in Great Britain and in the USA in 2012 by
Frances Lincoln Children's Books, 74-77 White Lion Street, London N1 9PF
www.franceslincoln.com

First paperback published in Great Britain and in the USA in 2015

PJJ
MORGAN
ANGIE

A CIP catalogue record for this book is available from the British Library.

ISBN 978-1-84780-463-1

Illustrated with pastels, watercolour and collage

Set in Mega LT

Printed in China

1 3 5 7 9 8 6 4 2

Daisy's BIG DIG

ANGIE MORGAN

F

FRANCES LINCOLN
CHILDREN'S BOOKS

I'm Daisy and I live at Number One, Magnolia Street with my mum and dad and Monty, my dog.

I like talking to EVERYONE on our street. But do you think they talk to each other?

No, they don't!

At Number Two lives old Mr Hofmeister.
He's about a hundred and if he had a sign on his door
it would say **KEEP OUT** in big, black, spiky letters.

He has an enormous garden where he grows fantastic
vegetables. Even I eat Mr Hofmeister's vegetables
and I hate vegetables.

At Number Three live the Daves:
Big Dave, Small Dave and Smiley Dave.

They're students so their garden is extremely messy.
Mr Hofmeister calls them rude names. But I like them.

Big Dave helped me with my homework once.
I got a star AND a smiley face.

At Number Four live the Lemming family.
Mrs Lemming has LOADS of children.

It's always noisy and Mrs Lemming says,
"All I really want is a bit of Peace and Quiet."
She never gets it, though.

My best friend is Lucy Lemming.
She comes to my house a lot.

She says I'm really lucky to have
a room of my own. She has to share
with her brother, Milo, who picks
his nose and has a tarantula.

At Number Five live Tarquin Fanshawe and his mum and dad.

Tarquin is never allowed out in case he gets dirty or catches something.

He reads all the time and he hasn't even got a TV.

At Number Six lives old Mrs Benjamin.
She makes brilliant cakes and her house always
smells of cooking. She's nearly always smiling
but she sometimes gets sad.

Her daughter and all her grandchildren live in
Australia, which is on the other side of the world.
We've got a globe in our classroom.
That's how I know.

Professor Flowerdew and his wife live
next to Mrs Benjamin at Number Seven.

Professor Flowerdew invents things.
Once he blew up his shed trying to
invent a new kind of electricity.

The fire brigade had to come.
It was brilliant.

One day I went round to see old
Mr Hofmeister and he was very worried.
He'd hurt his back lifting a very large
marrow, and now he couldn't dig
his garden.

I wanted to help, so I said, "Don't worry,
Mr Hofmeister. Leave it to me."

I needed a plan,
so I went to find Lucy.

We had a think.

Then we had a snack.

Then we had another think and
we came up with a GOOD PLAN.

We wrote lots of letters.
They said:

Mr Hof~mxe~ister would
like to invite you
to A
DIGGING PARTY
on Saturday afternoon
There will be tea and cakes
p.s There is also hidden treasure.

And then we posted them to all our neighbours.

Everyone came!

Mr Hofmeister was a bit surprised when they all arrived at his house.

But lots of INTERESTING THINGS happened.

The Daves did most of the digging and Mr Hofmeister had to admit that their digging was the best.

He said he would give them lots of vegetables, which would be good for their brains.

Tarquin and Professor Flowerdew got on like a shed on fire!

They didn't dig much.

$$x^2 \times y^3 + \left(5 - \frac{9}{23}\right)^3$$

Mrs Benjamin had a really good time digging with the Lemming children.

Mrs Lemming kept saying, "Do let me know if they're a nuisance."

She didn't mean it though. She was enjoying the Peace and Quiet.

Everyone loved the tea and cakes.

And what happened
after the party?
Well.

Mrs Benjamin had the Lemming children round to her
house a lot and they baked cakes and made things,

and Mrs Lemming FINALLY
got some Peace and Quiet.

Tarquin was able to borrow loads of
interesting books from Professor Flowerdew,
but his mum never let him go in his shed
(just in case of explosions).

Mr Hofmeister and the Daves became good friends, and the Daves did really well at their exams because of eating all those vegetables.

And was there any treasure in Mr Hofmeister's garden?

What do you think?

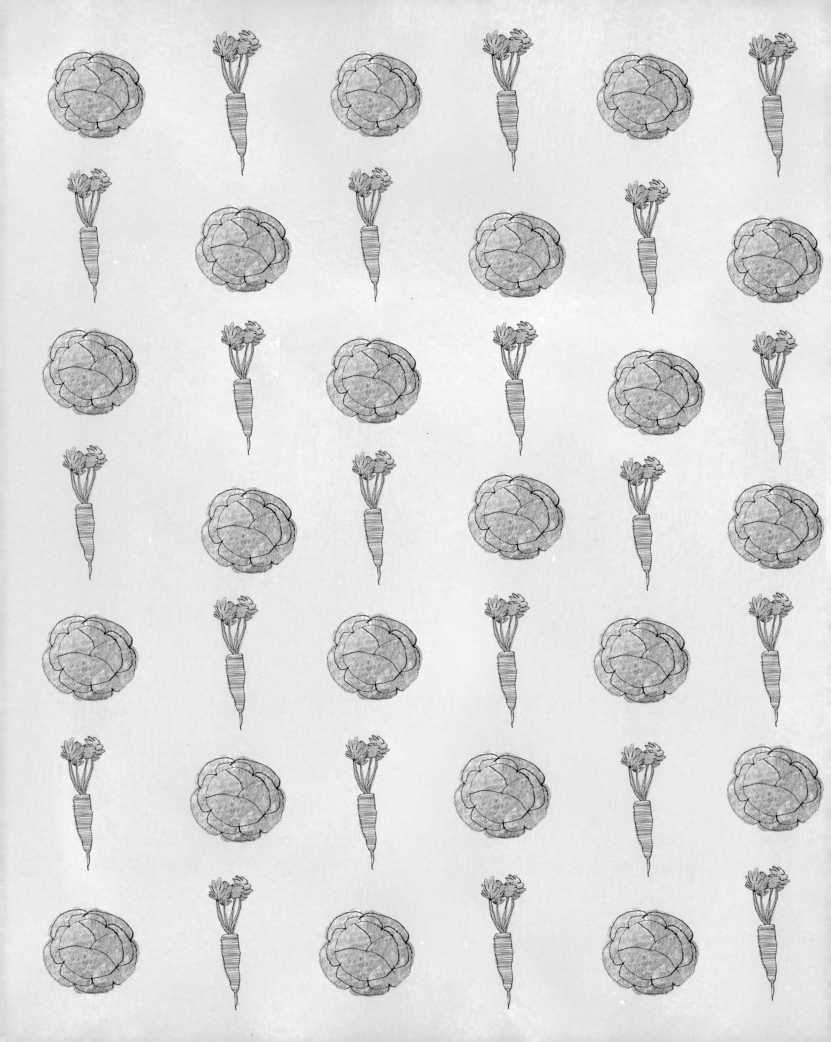

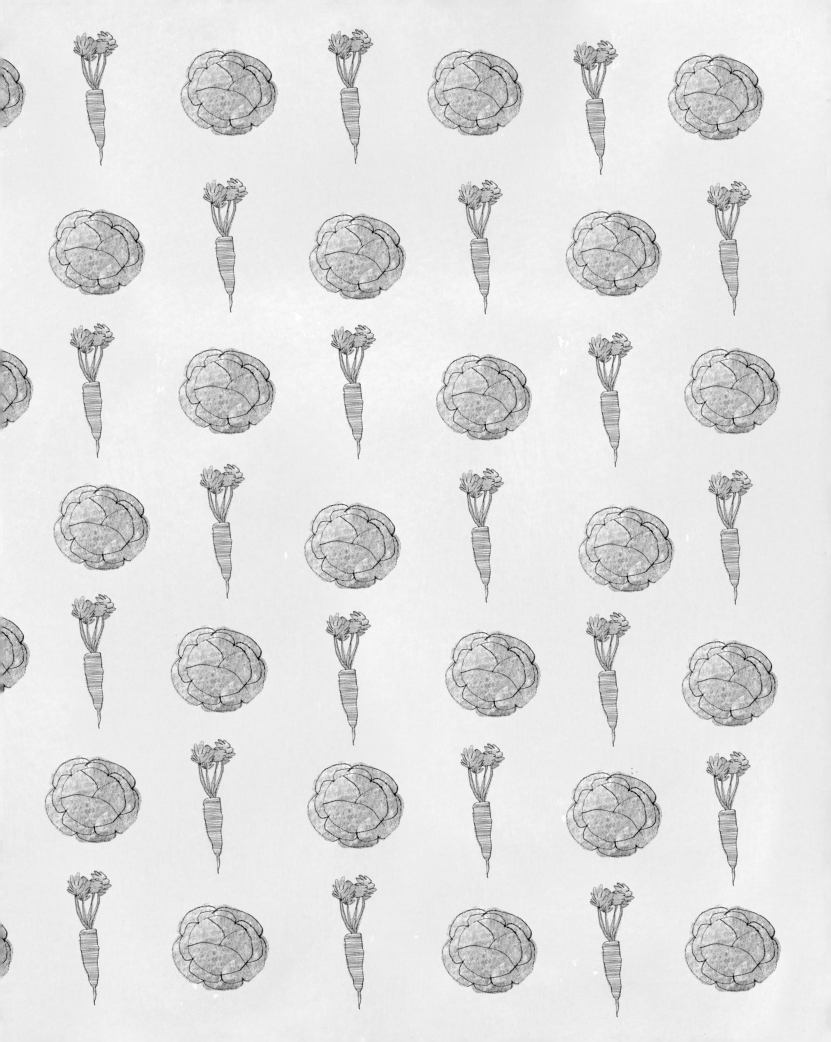

ALSO BY ANGIE MORGAN
PUBLISHED BY FRANCES LINCOLN CHILDREN'S BOOKS

ENORMOUSE

978-1-84780-526-3

Enormouse is bigger than all the other mice in the mousehole – and he looks different too.
He is teased by the other mice, even though he takes care of them, and when the mice find
a picture of a rat they all decide that Enormouse is actually a rat.
Poor Enormouse leaves the mousehole and goes to join the rats. But what he discovers is
that looks aren't everything. The rats are dirty and untidy, and he is not at all like them.

Now he realises where his true home lies...

Meanwhile the mice have also realised their mistake. They miss Enormouse and set out on
a dark and dangerous journey to find their friend and bring him home.

Frances Lincoln titles are available from all good bookshops.
You can also buy books and find out more about your favourite titles,
authors and illustrators on our website: www.franceslincoln.com